RAPUNZEL

Manufactured in U.S.A. for the publishers Peter Haddock Ltd. Bridlington, England.

ISBN: 0 7105 0751 8

Cover Illustration by Phil Wilson

Illustrations by Phil Wilson

Contributing Writer: Bette Killion

KT-494-952

John and his wife Nell lived in a cottage in a small village. More than anything, they wished for a child. Next door lived a wicked witch named Helga. She had a house with a big garden. Helga wished for a child, too.

One day, Nell had a sign that she would have a baby. That same day, she saw some rapunzel lettuce growing in the witch's garden. It looked so green and fresh. Nell cried, "I must have some of that lettuce."

John loved her so much that he picked some of the lettuce for her. But Helga came upon John picking her lettuce.

"How dare you steal my rapunzel!" the witch screamed. "You will both pay for this!"

John explained about his wife's hunger for the lettuce. Helga answered, "Very well. Take all the rapunzels you like. But when the baby is born it will be mine."

John was so upset that he agreed. Nell ate a lot of rapunzel lettuce, and soon a beautiful little girl was born to them. She had blue eyes and golden blonde hair. They loved her at once.

The next day, Helga came and claimed the child as her own. John had to be true to his promise, so Helga took their child away. She named the baby Rapunzel and took her to a faraway place to live.

Rapunzel's thick, golden hair grew fast and long and, as she grew, she became ever more lovely.

One evening, when Rapunzel was twelve years old, Helga used her powers to call the great Raven of the North. She told him to carry Rapunzel away to a high tower in a forest. The Raven did as he was told. Helga was waiting for them at the tower. She imprisoned Rapunzel in the tower, which had no doors or stairs and only one chamber at the top.

Rapunzel was frightened when the witch went away. But the Raven stayed through the first night and made soft sounds to soothe her. He felt sorry for Rapunzel but he had no powers of his own. He could not break Helga's will.

The next morning Rapunzel heard Helga calling her from outside the tower.

"Rapunzel, Rapunzel,
Let down your hair."

Rapunzel wound her long tresses around a hook next to the window and let down her hair. It looked like spun gold in the sunlight. Helga caught the strands in her hands and climbed up into the tower. She stayed with Rapunzel only a short time, bringing food and water.

Every morning Helga came and called to Rapunzel and every morning Rapunzel let down her long hair. But Rapunzel was still lonely. She made friends with the birds who flew by her window and they taught her to sing beautifully. She spent many hours singing to the forest animals.

The rabbits, the foxes, the deer—even the bears and the wolves—loved to hear Rapunzel singing. Wherever they were in the forest, they would stop and listen to her beautiful voice.

Some days, the squirrels or a raccoon might climb up the tower wall and bring Rapunzel some nuts or a juicy apple.

A little bluebird came every morning to perch on Rapunzel's windowsill. Rapunzel named her Sky because she was as blue as the sky and because she was as happy as a little sunbeam. Every morning Sky sang with Rapunzel and then quickly flew away just before Helga arrived.

When Rapunzel had been in the tower for a long, long time, a handsome prince came riding through the forest. He was on a mission for his father, the king. Suddenly, he heard a beautiful voice singing somewhere among the trees. He guided his horse toward the enchanting sound. When he got closer, the singing stopped and a harsh voice called,

"Rapunzel, Rapunzel,
Let down your hair."

The prince was amazed to see the beautiful, long hair and the ugly witch climbing up. He wanted to hear the girl sing again, but the witch stayed. The prince promised himself that he would return and rode on to fulfill his mission.

As the prince rode back through the forest on his way home, he came again to the tower. All was quiet. He walked to the foot of the tower and called as he had heard Helga call,

"Rapunzel, Rapunzel,
Let down your hair."

Rapunzel came to the window, but she hesitated because the voice was strange. When she saw the prince, she let down her hair and the prince climbed swiftly to her window.

"Sing for me!" he begged her. Rapunzel was so happy that she sang more sweetly than ever before.

Every day after that the prince climbed up to see Rapunzel. And every day she sang for him.

One day, Helga arrived at the tower earlier than usual. As she came near, she heard Rapunzel singing. The song was so sweet that Helga knew something was different.

She crept close to the tower and watched. Soon she saw Rapunzel say good-bye to the prince. She watched him climb down from the tower on the golden hair and ride away into the forest.

"Someone has tricked me!" Helga screamed.

She dashed home without leaving the food and water for Rapunzel. Back in her own house she stormed and stomped and shrieked that someone was trying to take her own, beautiful daughter away from her.

When evening came, Helga summoned up all her powers and called the great Raven of the North.

"Take them both!" screamed Helga. "Fly them to the poorest, most miserable country you can find and leave them there. They will be unhappy all their lives!"

As the Raven reached the tower, the two were escaping from the tower on Rapunzel's hair. She had cut it off and tied it to the window hook. The Raven grasped Rapunzel and the prince in his claws and started for the far country. The two held each other close and Rapunzel, still happy to be with her prince, began to sing.

The sound was so beautiful that it melted the Raven's heart. It gave him the strength to break Helga's will.

The Raven flew both of them straight to Rapunzel's first home. John and Nell were overjoyed to see their beautiful daughter and the prince.

Soon after, the prince and Rapunzel were married. They all went to live in his father's castle, far away from the wicked witch.